POPULAR FICTION
JAMES SHERRY

ROOF

Special thanks to the editors of the following magazines where some of this work originally appeared: *Alembic, Assassin, Benzene, Chicago Review, Ironwood, Island, New Observations, Oink, Paris Review, Poets' Encyclopedia, Sun & Moon,* and *Zone. Integers* was performed as a collaboration with dancer, Nina Wiener, at Dance Theatre Workshop.

ISBN 0-937804-15-0
Library of Congress Catalog Card Number 85-61017

Photograph of the author by Cheung Ching-Ming
Production by Diane Ward

ROOF BOOKS
are published by
The Segue Foundation
300 Bowery
New York, N.Y. 10012

Table of Contents

E P I S T L E
A P O L O G Y

Riding from the capital to my home in New York, I noticed that autumn was still intense here in the south and I thought to write a poem, a posteriori, that would, by its rhythms transmit the rush and transition of the season, but full of regrets for not having been able on my trip to formulate or remember answers to certain questions that had been put to me about myself and my work, I am attacked by anxiety that the placid beauty of leaves changing color out the window of the train cannot alleviate. All the pieces are present; I have merely to put them together with procedures that. . . or are the procedures laid out yet.

Autumn is when leaves get very colorful as they are dying, a high culture phenomenon. The remnants and abilities—profundity, rationality, spontaneity—have a great impact on the senses, but because what will happen soon is so obvious that it's not really threatening, except through fear of change, most remain increasingly calm throughout. And it's not a mistake either to go about our business or to shape what was too unformed to emerge this season into a thought that can be stated next spring when we have another chance to reach more people.

With certain friends I feel compelled to know more about myself and to express it more clearly than I would or even feel is true. The brilliant propositions distilled from years of labor that seem to abound in the great literary, scientific and philosophical works of the past, but are more simply perceptions of particulars, are too far away to be grasped completely in every conversation and in any case can

5

only come out from an explanation of how I feel in all my inconsistancies about a given topic and this itself, which I often don't want to admit, incites my mind to riot away from forthrightness which is its refuge.

These breath of autumn thoughts, mutated into strange shapes by generations or a nodding acquaintance with someone somewhat beyond critical mass, do not have the clarity and impact of the leaves peaking, and I feel more comfortable, that it is scaled, as I ride to where the leaves are all on the ground and the branches up in the air. It is less exciting, but to speak nature as well as the honed abstractions of native discourse is to remember all the dialects.

On the other hand I can only convince by being myself. The rough edges showing in the thought in the rhetoric is a way out of the abysses of mind and aids insofar as communication is possible. The notion is elitist, but I don't think that the elites will support it either just yet. This is because a multiplicity of languages, as distinct from a universal language, which by now can be seen as praxis, includes science and technology languages, genre languages written in detective novels and science fiction, Black English, even literary language, that is, all one thinks to say in the way one thinks it, and as such is a recursive concept the ruling class cannot sustain.

To accept that complexity does not have to be unified or that unification is packaging language for consumption is to understand both the plan and the intention. To skirt an issue to give it credibility and leave a hole where itself is and assume that will be seen as intended is an aesthetic that can only survive in its nest, impossible outside of art, although I am here pointing to where this started.

A B O U T

This is about about, until now a subject reference, point of interest or city all roads converged upon. This is about about; to say what it's about and to be about it on all sides, around its house, in circuit, around the outside, here and there, approximately, almost, also includes a reversed position, in rotation, colloquially, near, in the vicinity, all round, in the neighborhood, not far from, on the verge of as a gerund (about being), concerning, but no longer "the subject" or what it's "about", more in the original sense of outside. It is the indexed subject, a space of nouns, persons in action, the words that pertain to their vicinity and intention or set them off by opposition. Space is made for a subject by delineating around it. The subject is what's left over: Not the thing, but what's about it.

Such non-referential and abstract modes express characteristics; for example, beauty is about ends, the spaces between our points of view, that is, about the corruption that fosters it—a possibility not out of line with traditional notions of transience. This is presented as an alternative to narrative creation, clothes that do not fit or are artified to appear to fit. The emperor's new clothes concealed nothing, and one can see now he is naked.

PRINCE
VALIANT

Drum up bangs. Moat foot, deliver. Imperium Wordium is charade who(se) applause go over.

I'd too places. Phone Foil-voice? Stop loving my atrocities.

Hunger for mere sepulchral foregone. Grind wonder: what-look-shake / (remove two as obviate). Let : comit to I.D. Hair up you tell me you're who hair down? Short of breat. *Not* looking at me?

Summer evening with mouth

Summit of manners to get rid of you.

*I*taly, *V*audeville, *D*evotion; row row row. Try unbusiness. (They can't believe we'd try offense.)

In the act of despairing go moribund: S.S. France, mignon — industry of arms in the wings of your blueprint.

Make = 's sign. All we HAVE in mind, frog for kiss.

hard, camp, post, Celt-woebegone. Coughs the merry boat girl singular. . . . Pitted swords recall withdrawing Romans. Too late for code : Defense. Reason hold that line. Half-nelson aorta. We have something more to say.

wavering — if you do not; you know th' castle will fallen. Star (leather bound). music laugh-lit. . . committ.

Gift of your half-eye. Colored ribbons hello. referred harmony. gill life.

Begin with state of nary: elephant, dance orient, owed government, hold my vote, warming over defeated intravenously.

Votary, salttooth, bal masque. Tall, straight, moral, a give.

Liars all adjectives the lady ladrone Ladino lading, life-boat with wheels, birth noise more exculpate. Dr. on skis (narrative) gimme.

Swill veritas mordant. Red list you serious. Socializing condones no merit, harvest, frugality, planting charts, there's no question of success.

I get white during working hours. Sleeve silence, dark capital, L dicta, so she can: a. drink   b. a cup.

vibration communion record vanquish fat dank imposition, pure stops rain soldier. hawk a mural / the comrade drink, color vitality, lost red kerchief of seer,

II.

Smoking ruins, battleaxe dangles. You want to continue so. She emptied the can of Hunt's Tomato Paste with a teaspoon. Foci of an ellipse (back formation, defect).

Who are you anyway that I should be more than polite? So classic she expressed nothing, thankyou. Correspondence zero, to you, two front teeth. Look and fled.

Can we begin to hug soon? (The final finish is straight grain.) Pleasure, arm, length and long feet constructivist. . .

He stepped on her in his boredom, in the museum of hysterics, gaucho, a good sportsman interested in scores.

In our eyes we are entirely in the sun, but in our sex we'd better go to the beach. He wired himself together after a night in the mead hall.

Too late (as in sure) for the mule. Spit on his hands, the handle slipped strangely. Photocopies of my . . . Ordinary, drill, melodramatic, many baskets for one fruit, I have more (wanting what was wit or humbleness). . .

At this point the Rhinemaidens felt it was time to go home. They crouched around the fire facing their hands.

The only score / / (slashes) were her knees. A square of stairs patterns future stars.

Next time I'll be entirely soothing, a blam to your abraded senses and full of praise. The friendly Samoan kissed her cheek, exhaling under the buttons of her blouse, a chain of pice around his neck; poet's spring in degree days. The four part musical structure betrayed her — mavin, mabinogi — (and this is only the haircut).

As ran out of time he had to, she moves better to the left. I'd like to say one thing at a time: Approach, inspect, ponder and develop smaller fragments.

Restraint recognizes it's understudy, unsay.

A nun expects charity. Princely enclosure. Too good-hearted to give her any expectations; Give me your tires, your port.

Suddenly she drew a deep breath and began to speak freely — You've made a rope of words and strangled this business. 80% of it will go for taxes. I'd say give me a minute, but. . .

Broadway AND Hollywood, like a nylon lemon peel, Kell the people, that lack of pretense, understanding, a protective feeling, I started concocting a little plot of my own.

So attractive that she really FELT what she said. And Childebert chopped up Clovis and Clovis chopped up Alaric.

Now that my brothers are dead the entire kingdom belongs, sending reports full of untruths. (Pandora: what they call Job's development. (Men have been hanged for less.))

Three or four years passed. . . A.D. 340, Council of Gangres, Canon 14: And if I come a step closer, take off your shoe and clunk me over the head with it.

She went to the king in a raging temper, determined to disinherit her daughter for all share in her father's property. The main cause was Rignuth's habit of sleeping with all and sundry. There are no examples of humor in Books I–IV.

Let's shake hands again. Dart into talks.

Throughout his youth — in jousts, at swordplay, in the race — his only thought was how to be admirable. Then they got a couple of pruning hooks and fished me out. Connect the dots and find the monkey.

A third time the Saxons came forward, offering all their clothes, their cattle and the whole of their property. 1400 years later Clermont-Ferrand had become headquarters of the Maquis.

I don't even know what I'd do with you if I had you. That night Val sent a secret message to their camp, "Come at once."

III.

Mute spells throat of, pawned (giveaway). You mean phone?

An-other Bride of Flowers. Foot / mouth = foot / shin . . . unwebbed, concoct A.D.

Manifestly tangent, frothing stones, sweep them to England. A screen for GET ON that screens devotion. When you DON'T.

Give 'em no chance, overwhelm and retreat to a coy — get grift and given. (Say whatever you want won't do.) Ravening enclosed. Hoping by portray to squelch: Noblesse manque.

Why not terrorism? Why not terror? Letters of your name especially spaced: Moult, multo, mulatto (I boiled your old skin.)

Serious? Yesterday's bread. Rooms of light we left. Forbidden ground — what will not support life (two kinds of mothers). Instant token, vehicle of sentiment. A place where I've lived and you come from.

Say I want: 29 Tue 30 Wed, sired power had not put away the thought. Incredibly effort to fail, onboard amusements, the sleeve from France, turnbuckles pulley.

Chiropodist. Colander. To let yourself out: ten grams and 10 grams and ten grams. Earth, hearth, household snake. Oddly refine technique, anachronistic

Not much experience of life? — All those years freshening up, cultivating ideals, supralapsarian formulae, meet on green. Bower block. Friday. Your afternoon house. Your evening house. People glued by habit. Petals welded by spells. Incantation. Panoply. Cardamom. Betrays use this key to leave.

She made him look at the birdie. Simurgh. Let him have. Short

12

flight after ash, best mad, solitary on a flat rock. Then I remade:

Bulging barrow baked in a boiled sun. Herself white as a sheet made pretense to herald the games spent on broken prey.

Honor of sundered, moor grey fair hound, on deck roundel, PYX, image, doubt, of dreadful, trance. Naked at the wedding feast.

Primarily fissure with that coiffure. "Don't scare me." Plain of Europe gripped by. Can't we just? "Drum them to the sea."

Crenelated efforts to. Break into your absent armory. Where late Gallo-Romans protected from hairy Princes by divine sanctions...

Let me explain: It isn't that I wanted to not, thus, my. (Nuptial wafer, wine absorbed.) Has change REALLY? I COULD have. I depreciated.

Sacrement define a mouth? Perennial. Pet cock?, no, peteman. Duplicitous twig.

Treaty of mutual resistence. Whispers in trowel... Empty contents, extrude...

...Jack-in-the-box! Come-on, shake. Prepare to hold. Speech between words. For who blew what?—Hammer to discover if I'm occupied.

Anxiety, of excess punctuation. Facts of (your) life. Through grid. Arm through. Offered through portcullis. Imprint of, on my chest. Saved by...so in future funnies, let a furtive hand, a chopped hand, a drawn hand never flexed. Safe art hand?

Trees Alsatian schoolboys to from. Tribe b(r)ought. Shuffleboard. Requiem for seems. Val's secrets...

Paper folded near the grate; breakfast to look. Fantasy schooling.
Galahad bandaids. vague vain votary voluptuous w. x. Recurs, horse
savages, edifice to.

NOTHING

That of which many large varieties are found in the major cultural centers of the United States. Although the eminent Earl of Rochester, John Wilmot, has somehow ascertained that Nothing was the elder sibling of Shade and spoke to it as to a familiar, the more modern variety seems unrelated to anything in particular, itself derived from nothing and going in that direction from which it came.

Nothing, as implied above, is derived from nothing, although translators of Hindu and Buddhist literature have more often found nothing to be a prefix of Ness, unrelated to the Scottish monster, which is only nothing coincidently. In colloquial terms nothing is what one has "plenty of", and it would not behoove any compilation of contemporary learning and culture to omit.

Nothing has been called dust, void, eternity, but in reality shirks all these aliases in modern times as being metaphysical, preferring the contemporary tendency to ascribe importance to the particular and objective; hence the modern tendency to make it a noun or person, making light of it by "little" or much of it by "big", the latter of which in this increasingly hectic age has tended to thrive more than the former.

FALLS

Worth poaching for congruence, dirty hands, the transition to new fruitless understanding. While drinking heavily, do not rely on ancestors' consistency. Directing their steps downward, industrial slavery at the highest level and a clod of a chaplain are all ringside, training such emotions that actually arise from the knowledge of an advantaged tuber.

This method and trial and error on intuition to conduct a tiptoe through legit labyrinths, isolated by thinking oneself all around ill-chosen objects of affection, appearance no longer when beer, might have made quite a surface nervousness had not the populace declared itself.

Instinctual entertainment, illustrated by individual actualities in vivisection and dime cash, discovered with earth colors, satisfying those requirements is really pleaded. You say but but, but there is really no substitute for the feeling of release, when the rope knotted so veins behind your back bulge, but you wriggle free.

Bones jellifying, swim through the light, grasp her hair and, boat drifted off, set out swimming toward sunset as opposed to plotting yourself through a fallow field and marking off an arbitrary outline for size. Start digging at the circumference or work out on foibles or control, making fun of the lowliness of our Savior.

The multiple forms being perceives disclose the happy balance attained in culminating the adventures and experiments set into geometry, y in place of x which is y + you, and the figure front in these forms when their stuffing so rots that the acrylic fur peels away from personal modesty, transforming almost as you look at it under which the earth is full of stones.

* * *

When I turn, he'd be lost, regions of story beyond, enjoyed through New England by hand. A final ballot to remove you have my complete assurance that I will introduce no feelings of impenetrable discrepancy (it's in the mail) from Hellenic mentality and medieval scholasticism.

Her bust, the fish in the road, contradicts the spot assigned to me by rage against regions of tangents constructed by bohemian existence, balk, guilt ethic enough until the six o'clock news, but I dragged you anyway to a tryst in a tutu, more concerned with who you were than the business of stuffing garbage cans with what might have been.

In the first place, let G, Y, C and F be given points. They are located on a woman and supply a unique opportunity for scientific examination was meant to be believed, enchanted, whereas this compass might quibble, although the curve is of the second class.

Those who find belief difficult screech at their foundation. Illusion days that come again is universal. Opinions contain truth, nor which in various ways, reasoning when I grabbed easy to follow remains until you find out something about it, no inkling what you wanted, knowing what I wanted was base and repulsive to human habits and proclivities. You insisted it couldn't be that bad and demanded to know. Then you got a queer look like Swiss nobility.

The most unreasonable things in the world can be made to appear reasonable by the application of reason. The liason officer is solemn and covered with decorations. The world, unaware and well in hand, curls into a ball and sleeps. The rest of us have a good old time.

17

DISINTERMENT

Producify by exclusioness
give by subvert
replumb or dismake shiftment
submonition to Thursday

Dismorphology   Unheraldrate
rememberment   deassurify

Ok to refriend (stamp)
depertinent takeability
unmongst
rephrasatory unfemalization

Disregard, recoriate pairitude
comparement of sculpturority: defile (side) vs.
unremergement as selfification
safed to suspiciate, not reever, simplicon of nonfinement

uncontinued deferral of reselfizationicity
cat-meow yellowize
unregenerate redigressivity
unlistening, hand descention from wrist
prechandelierizement digiticity
deconnoiter hydromarinertudinousness
foppitude respite feminotropicity
desophisticate identizoid — African sculptines

WEST INDIES
EXERCISE BOOK

Apart from the Barthian deviation of genre writing, taking over the universal bourgeois writing style or language in 19th century Europe...

Can we reconstruct by coalition genres, interlocking genres, substitutions of words from one genre's vocabulary into the kinds of sentence structures of another, stereo thinking in one genre on two thoughts, stereo writing in several genres on one thought, extension of normative grammar as a genre, e.g., using sentence structure as a genre, extending the possible 'correct' sentence structures to include several sentences linked by commas or two thoughts linked as if they were one by normative grammar, or 'correct' sentences that do not really become a full thought until they have grown into a paragraph. Or using the paragraph as the repository for a single thought, determined by metrics or tones of vowels or becoming 'clear' only after several such sentences have been compounded.

What genres can go together? How many are necessary to make universal language? What is synergy here?

Can we revert to 19th century language by imbuing the genre with thought and details of uncertainty that imply a systematic process behind the apparently limited genre or is that retrograde and academic—the alternative being additive and synthetic—grammar and content?

How can we show the relationship of extended grammars and layered genres except by making it meaningful? (This writing as philosophical genre of meditation (but fiction 'cause of my elliptical mentality.))

Can uncertainty become a mechanical and neurotic process? Only reasoning within the discipline (as Wittgenstein says yellow-green with respect to yellow & green and blue-green and yellower-green, etc; as Greenberg says self critical art) can supply the assurances needed to believe what one says although some will be swayed by delivery, flash value, occasional revelation as opposed to continuous revelation of closely festooned trains of thought. But these too are suspect as derivative or constricted as opposed to journalistic revelation of 'fact' (supposed fact) after fact to create a simulacrum of reality — style, transparency through which the world of politics or sex can be seen as it 'really' is.

Genre writing as all other 'modern' art contains a substrate of satire. If we apply high taste, e.g., not too many adjectives, not too much sensationalism in action or language, then we satirize our own intentions because we apply such seriousness to Flash Gordon or Lew Archer. If we apply standards of genre taste, e.g. 'letting the good times roll', we satirize our own desire to 'get down' and sensationalize. Only multiplicity can be 'radical' enough to subdue the 'fact' that we know too much (late-city man, ennui, etc.) and send us tumbling into a state where we realize we have to be prepared to learn something totally new. But the problems of multiplicity.

There is no way to objectify the relations between sensations or styles because there is no between. Between objects there are other objects. Between them others down to mote objects and so to massless bodies. Objects of attention (affection) describable as plasmas of varying densities. Mix societies but focus attention where we will — not taste again — and that becomes the object and then objects and so the modernist attempt to focus on the objective between sensa-

20

tions, e.g., existence, transition. Paradox of this kind of thinking if done in minimal terms.

But as our presence is combinative....

So Mondrian talks about relations between sensations. What are they? This is met as a proposal. In terms of perceptions—it is ambiguous, but in terms of art, it is descriptive because art has clearly divisible parts that set up relationships. How can one associate them? Is that fetishistic?

(Color is additive: Gestalt sensations arise when the parts are tightly bound. Some configurations are dominated by wholeness. Others tend to separate into parts. The process of composition in genre is to combine the parts in such a way that they both create a family and fall into parts, parts that relate to their original nature and parts that are combinative.)

Working with the Gestalt, not of regular forms, but of irregular, complex, ungraspable forms. How can this Gestalt be shaped? Worked? Worded? Extend the faculties for recognizing such shapes —sculptural writing.

"S A Y 'C H E E S E'"

Say you got a boot open, but believe in them. Somnambulance is no conk.

Unparallel equal signs, a three-star bog, could've flushed.

Go flat for the stop light. Is that all? Despair boys, digest it first, of the opening road.

Stately would be nice after tv poses weekend, conceit, freedom, tarantula, conversely reads practice.

Inflammatory materials *only*: yes no yes no rerun helix beddybye confuted, *all* there to be slower configuration, seeing it *work* it out, thee in thou, inside out goes far without mirror to view rears. Don't know or *have* to know, but inside is what's called 'friendly' advice.

Latin quarry to act this postpaid harm or pain to say no, i.e., "NO", momentarily absolute shrinks. No, expedient *or* see much. AND, risk it lovable adverb this much outright. Separate and separates. Fictive heart concerned with thicker. . .

'Good luck' (?) Progress perfectly fueled for stranger. Fold of sleaze. Come to with flimsy-sudden.

'Whatever you say.' Look at *what* and know which is up / eviscerated. Were right, are right, beginning. Now *excuse* . . . ,

That or what felt.

Stirs. Get *through*, got to to mean, too, to *mean* to get through.

Sleeper a stringpiece; outside the door get a presence, dotted line around, toll, bodies. Sensitive was when, now sense, among which is the former.

Trademark of soap unlaminates surfaces, peso back, frog skin, shrivelled into determination after pitch or ring. Back there?

Cool out one for you, one for me, one postcard what flinch for inward. Coast, pedal, along the coast.

Curbist question wants money and / over smiles. Thought everything. Bag, absolute, worse, balk, balk, bald.

Early tossing, literal as 'solutions', say 'freeze', not saying it, what to do with it; what else but genre-life, meat of potatoes.

Sacred texts substitute for sacred texts.

Brakeless on seeing too as arrive too slow, at once, and again borrow, out of this, to do it to get it to do otherwise than.

Punctuation not less sufficient bake book, cobwebs rid of alcove.

Peace with piece, neither works, peeling bacon slices. Philosophical concerns slugs military primogeniture allocate.

Drips linkage rush regret restore alternatives direction fruition heresay heresy bad jazz all on the-that.

Invent it or can you / it.

Interrupting plus try holding patter; give it away, get, push now, I'm as you, which it, what, there was no reason to be otherwise, if will to let it be what it had to or else it wasn't as it is, folly of its own rhetoric.

More touchy, are limit traces ant-hill grace.

Any always. . .donations, present, perfect unreasonableness. Chic cliche.

Estuary at an angle. Laced housing. Whistle, mail, respite, leather mommy. The rest on your doorstep shows no shoe.

Brassy late appointment. Golden unilateral dismemberment, dignifying zilch, possesses beliefs. Dead and red. Herring.

Superstition names interlock.

Dropping cherries domain cosseted orchid. Lay around using items like long-green eyes.

Cleaning having lost the rug. One thing or two about kneading, says madness left.

Father to further social incontinence, a wet-back apricot needed all their warnings—bosomy colonel's widow, lunkish pols, snake-bird saves only once. Clunk / night.

As states caffeined roach velvet, anyone who has a heart enjoys Italy. Two-dupes take-out. Dig out, well busy with moody, wilting carefully.

Chair possessed anyway passport. Adios Luxor. Procure slow or never poised on each fill, in filling. . .out.

Report metempsychosis; trust alm-chair alternative, walk-on in a film about rice-fields. Trading down much? Commitmentabilia.

With head get a free glass, laundry dusk urge / usage.

Bargaining for licks evaporates mutual interest, it fooling crowd of poets, nervous stand-ins, leaving to leave, cop to romance.

Noise pure-as-dull. No one's fooling oneself.

Pleasant solo have piazza steps horrors of night ass value, theory frontiers then 'drinky'.

Diary notices eclipsed: wine-clavicle lastly smelled dusty. Inevitably blame / blameless.

Nomenclature lapse to discovery.

I felt, I felt and then I felt decade. I can guess wrong. I have. Arabian bites disattribute stroll distinctives. Could have had. No keep no. Tryst-superstition. Flunky til cat dies ha-ha. Ignore them numbers.

Realize equals lions tuned.

'Separate advantage.' Confronted swarthy remember. Desperate quarter.

Call this out soap yet? Say cheese this and then that, had it got it then then?

Personnel questions. Albedo. Look-kissed lineage.

Wife left husband-rights is a sentence to serve. After that he went bad.

Stable scent tipped a civil-state. Savant-hat on the wrong head. Huntress' thumb expressly devoid. Saying it out-politic.

Got a little repair, lady, in the veiled problem of classical research. Still, to tell, to early.

INTEGERS

I. Integers at Bay

Filch words. Wet like. Truss intelligence. Lawless potshards.
Checkered rate. Your floe. Key unruly. Lydian Dickens. Template
modes. Shadow poker. Over open. Likely fief. Pairing diagnosis.
Vertical pagination. Her slut. Smithian conclusive. More it. Fever
board. Polyglycoat nature. Rutting time. Imperium wordium.
Slavery pause. That _____. Suppresses goes? And on. Arithmetic
surge. Some there. Or : ram. Oak spif. Pier pair. Oaf line. Women
liberate. Met set. Include one. Pants paunch. Pilot piduciary. Piute
if. You just. Build death. Push opaque.

Garotte mystic velour. Lucky wire environs. Ignorant rectitude
succumbs. I'll wormwood migratory. Hack prairie breaker. Ibex
ward constabulary. Three word Walpurgis. Nice too is. Creeks plush
Ohio. Family gear pan. Thresh trap repeat. So says drape. Peer all
dust. We snuff parameters.

E're water it moves. Breathe pride and others. I jumped the
train. Stage planks the bone. Blue water over fade. Breathe out over
blue. We move its jump. Space over blue the. Pleasure in mutual
next. Attractive blue out space. Which breathe it moves. The water
of sand. Over move pride breathes. Which cloud wave sand. Sea-
scape punctuation e're I. Train to the breach. Aloes skin shades
refreshment. E're shift off cracks. Knit tires the sun. Space out over
blue. Blue's crack is horizon. Description surface ripples Orientalia.
What have I missed.

26

Please remember to keep clean. Safety valve with family support. A tinny subterfuge to avoid. Nelson, Richard, John, Paul, Ringo. We may find out soon. Come along, come along, Allen. Very kaolin to tell you. Blue army gall bladder fragments. The space of a pair. Pinch pink lying pink pinch. Nobody has time from to. Hypo, hypo, hypo, hypo, etc. Each last word mitigates mitigates. No jobs this week, weed. Alpaca mound presumes she'll let. Syntaxes, mellophone, allomorph conscientiously applied. Wee tooth in many dentistries. Hers senses ofs responsibilities errs. Modify grease, solvents, horizontal emblematic. Sir Gawain in green tights. America can't get enough of. . . You say you said it. The very Morse of it. Mortified trenchermen soupline the Indies. North reaches of the ankle. Allot fragments; ashamed he's scooped. Mach lorry can Mexico this. Meaning is transmitted through structure. Homer writers in such as. Lacquer cosine delete intension equals. Label octagonal stop natural sponge. Each card indispensible five stud. I like rain and sex. Steno rye on a slip. The oui can demand full. Having come this far step. Agile bucket conjures don envoy. Throttle adjacent k-ration degenerate op. By me that I took. Withall the easy it range. Along the fine blade attic. Suburban daguerrotypes isolate childhood embarrassment. One black, one brown shoe. Consulting paper then addresses now. Long has he walked upright. Laverne appears in a dream. So you will like it. First plural drumming underneath soundtrack. Morn etch cow hamper tile. Allah poule tint eighth contraption. Fuck u cn rd ths. Plaintain subway redoubt beside jealousy. To me in hoard lovers. Redolent up to the nose. Why am I doing this? Figure eights haggle each fetish. Mutually higgle, fives also tailgate. She balloons rug dust, Herbie. She corrects bleach and characterized. She unlaminated our good tub. Sandwiches rule broad finger counts. Include shadows — synonym: suggestive ornament. Translate without resorting as foreigners. Reubens will dispel small thoughts. Used words to gratify ego. Lose track more than five. Know how to find them. Among outer reaches of snapshots. This time to go now. Many definitions rain in conversation. I want to mean you. Leather gloves killed the effect. Sex used in literature to. Actual feeling of Bermuda Triangle.

II. Durations

1. Checkered rate, rut phase, slavery pause
   checkered game: help phase, regularly pause
   supernatural game: help supresses regularly claustrophobic

2. Lucky wire. Hack family, press length
   Peer wire   hack plush   three length
   peer too   inconstant plush   three trap

   push pour. tour serge. Ohio pressure
   push lush. Tour four. Ohio pliers.
   Crate lush. Alternate Four. Congruity pliers.

3. Anticipate succumbs. Ignorant drape. Construct demise.
   Anticipate push. Welling drape. Construct liberate.
   Constables push. Welling pull. Women liberate.

4. Humid way. Groat pride. Motorized fits.
   Oaf war. Enclosed pride. Motorized dust.
   Oaf hoof. Enclosed suction. Involved dust.

   Person anchor. Ooze grace. Express feelings.
   Person silo. Smooth grace. Touch feelings.
   Paunch silo. Smooth derelict. Touch especially.

5. like lady   quarters repeat   summoned formal   like gear

6. the / of / and / to / a / in / that / is / I / it / for / as /
   with / was / his / he / be / not / by / but / have / you /
   which / are / on / or / her / had / at / from / this / my /
   they / all / their / an / she / has / were /
   me / been / him / one / so / if / will / there / who / no /
   we / when / what / your / more / would / them / some / than /
   may / upon / its / out / into / our / these / man / up / do /
   like / shall / great / now / such / should / other / only /

any / then / about / those / can / made / well / old / must /
us / said / time / even / new / could / very / much / own /
most / might / first / after / yet / two // two / yet / after /
first / might / most / own / much / very / could / new / even /
time / said / us / must / old / well / mad / can / those /
about / then / any / only / other / should / such / now / great /
shall / like / do / up / man / these / our / into / out /
its / upon / may / than / some / them / would / more / your /
what / what / when / we / no / who / there / will / if / so /
one / him / been / me / were / has / she / an / their / all /
they / my / this / from / at / had / her / or / on / are / which /
you / have / have / but / by / not / be / he / his / was / with /
as / for / it / I / is / that / in / a / to / and / of /
the

7. Non-smokers permit   less pushby   throughout rice
   velour permit   less crush   throughout perpetuates
   velour skin   charade crush   heel perpetuates

8. Why leg work works deliberate

9. The foot   is parse   of bodies
   Profess foot   drunken parse   family bodies
   Profess steps   drunken steps   family steps

   Gorgeous preserved   return returns   continuous duration
   Gorgeous substitute   flyback returns   continuous go
   Include substitute   flyback associates   and go

10. Disco teethe   as armed   display us
    Disco Mohammed   as pumpkin   indistinct us
    Herd Mohammed   nice pumpkin   indistinct if

    Gratis bumper   deft clue   Mother code
    easy bumper   deft oleo   mother council
    easy vow   sumptuous oleo   slippery council

11. of / who / is / one / so / that

12. What might   droop suffix   ok angst
    we might   honor suffix   ok duck
    we plastic   honor air   dry duck

    Plural try(st)   hold damage   close brick
    plural soup   ear damage   relative brick
    molecular soup   ear out   relative stairs

13. to step the get get gets

14. Narrative lit   Blush contact   sully machine
    Blank lit   January contact   joint machine
    Blank line   January sump   joint active

    Lettuce crossing.   Jalopy gambol.   Symbiosis intimidates.
    Refinery crossing.   Casaba gambol.   Symbiosis consequence
    Refinery imbue   Casaba except   defile consequence

15. Sound track   sump her   remain coast
    need track   sump cohere   remain poultice
    Need fuel.   Assignation cohere.   Town poultice.

    Communion ribs.   Esoteric cross.   Subterfuge conglomerate.
    catching ribs.   esoteric that.   move conglomerate.
    catching effect   of that   move to

16. closure scenic   grid opened   what whatchamacallit
    closure hydrocarbons   exemplary opened   usury whatchamacallit
    awash hydrocarbons   exemplary sauced   usury overcast

    graphic privilege   launch aside   amenity preservation
    graphic presumptuous   assume aside   amenity perpetuates
    stage presumptuous   assume that   step perpetuates

17. step slide jump fall push pull support

III. Vowelic Integers

Deco epaulettes. Shakos oval. Hoping Polo. Grow soap. Noisy spin-
naker. Plead spiel. Repeat putt. Vagabond eatery. Uxorial disap-
pearance. Promulgate liner. Limes decode. Oblate inburst. Open
haze. Sweeten derange. As raptorial. Expect upbeat. Uvulate the.
Blue noon. Groucho pellegra. Range punitive. Past presence. Sim-
plified rancid. As flood. Minor minus. Minos deviates. Ole bread.

Albatross vertigo. Alligator mail. How white. Decipher mutual.
Outlet bandage. Connubial pugilist. We go. Let's conscript.
Furlough fricassee. Fresh frequency. Modulate modulates. Counter
fives. Prompt ye. He type. Older alphabet. Exigency aloft. Produce
errors. Thunder appointment. Jupiter rug. Adopt intercourse.
Punjab pollutant. Pike slip. Hold quick. Sepulveda Cheesemelt.
Notary publish. Alight pacemaker.

Wonder clover baseball. Mew wasp arrow. Weigh patient Tuesday.
Misinform float heel. Whale spaghetti chess. Fate elf fee. Loose tred
capon. Clovis faction pew. Myopic train fleet. Purloined Knievel
spout. Rumor poori semblance. Mulch envoy retribution. Sculptor
porter flight. Heavy loop caster. Export crematorium nudge. Solu-
tion deviate catatonia. Mistral corporation puck.

Knee wrench pleats. Decent gaggle sinecure. Everything silo but.
These of pledge. Such boss tone. X-ray figure yard. Meek gerund
highball. Hinny warmer equal. Otiose protagonist crows. Bound
croon humor. Tumult tuning tunicle. Crazy separates graze. Flay
laborer dedication. I I I. Cry decibels refund. Usury coordinate en-
comium. Obey five clothes.

Proprietary instincts reign. You flake cocoa. Mine gosling sensibility.
Case of it. Bite a magnet. So orphan novelty. Creak sterling gravy.
Cast of it. Greet scuffle meander. How to load. How toast poses.
How to procreate. We hear to. Juice silence ladder. Music ocher
pantry. As next pants. Yolk miserly jubilation.

IV. Transforming Integers

Camera closed in graffiti. Trees disclosed their shadows. Closure
there trees tether. So much pair whatsoever. Near closing shadow
him. Graffiti on their clothes. Close call there treat. The shade as
disclosure.

Pleasure drone sun through. Than man did so. Well in Albany
keeps. Giving us to submit. Man in the sun. Upstate in the well.
Drones hover and sow. Please in the keep. Drone of welling feelings.
Human two given rivers. Thorough about pleasing her. And keep-
ing to himself. The keeper main-man through. So pleasant they did.
Trust upstream and down. Give up his submissions.

The only external alarm. We'll leave you here. Only you alarm
through. The leaves we hear. Leave externals to me. Let's only alarm
them. Table leaf only you. Know is not alarming.

However intensely sensual hero's. He never gets her. She dies, he
works. A meatball hero gets. Tender or less sexy. Than a sausage
heroic. Heroine got no tense. As admirable as act. She however
works splits. His works tends harrowing. Sensitive tendrils get tangled.
Up in the narrative.

FLEECING

*"Alas! poor sheep! You will
always be sheared!"* —Beranger

Mall

Questionless motive (duck in pond); on the want market say anything.

What angel demolition team. That fret shorn.

Back and front to wall. Sanguine sanguinary.

Meanwhile continue without lives — a little fish and a little salad. The pitcher lacked likes the batter.

But if we are good, he is not us. Paki bashing. Equal rots.

A free license, taking my work off me for money. Moil of chickens.

Associative giggle. Last licks. To take to the cleaner, if you choose a la mode, again not or but and.

The construction of personality in order to . . . .

How the phone call peeled the onion for Herbie. Once upon it perch. Fireescape tomatoes.

To make her cat less hot. To run to fat to mean when the police are after you. What grammatical must rhetorical would. Plumwine substitutes for plumbline.

Sheer hype of forgetfulness to let her lie. There there. If you honestly want to know, No.

I will not give you a quarter reminds me of the time means took me for a bundle. Although adjacent to the summer Vatican, he ignores proximity. Causation first or last the way you're looking.

To avoid similar embarrassment, he spent most of the winter rubbing against a tree. Yes, I would like to, sometime.

To shave meaning by calling bushy tailed rodents 'tree rats' to inspire public opinion.

Make the proposition more enticing to turn pockets inside out; attribute necessity where it is possible to do otherwise, but a good buy is not to be ignored, garden variety.

Question the whole project of steps, hair, sanctuary, impulse, surveyor, eyeshade.

Who told Napoleon that a building is incessantly and continuously represented by a picture in the atmosphere, and that all existing objects project into that atmosphere a kind of specter which can be captured and perceived, and was subsequently consigned to Charenton, as Richelieu consigned Salomon de Caux for offering him navigation by steam? Whether as a thing or of a thing.

*

Theater, art, science, education tussle for authority to fleece the ambitious for pleasure, wealth, power, used by philosophers to fleece those who abstain from them. There is no perfect attitude. There is no tune. Another fiction tricks up. Illusion of tune.

Reason it. Fleeced. Suspiciously guard ourselves. Fleeced. Skepticism. Balded by shearers. Safe? So what. Let me be fleeced by thinking in other terms. Let this go.

He took it between his teeth then, but did not bite. Was she impressed? A tale told for telling, passive as nature.

He stuffed her hind legs into his high boots. I gave him my money to hold. I decided to sit down and write, because I like to see words pressurized off the keys.

Hired brains assume their attention to fine print and eagle feathers is more than fixation. Denuded by cancerous growth. "This is what is called social values of the supply side." —F. Nietzsche.

Well, we'll gaff other p.o.v., like baaa, like slurp, como...get to a rough place and put it down. Walk away with a shiver and a shrug.

*

The end of the phone call gets worse and I just got an Apache for the socially conscious—point of view expose. Neighborhood development benefits.

Don't make classical references, don't make fun of cripple: Jason limped passed to appear unthreatening. Resentment politics.

Mental energy remains in its unparsed state. To a monetary age, I left a tab a mile long. When in Rome, remain Greek. Opposition is an investment.

Meaning, the break even point, is never met.

Undoubtedly he had learned the worst: sharpen a pencil with a pencil sharpener and you betray humanity.

Anxiety that thinking exists. Idle fretting of the clock trying to sound sincere.

EMPHYSEMA

It shes fostered pardoning. Crisis folded is sleepy Japanese township songfest. Enlist avowal. Anxiety out. Along is crowded out.

Voting to writhe cloned bout now. Revert to problem solving soothing. If muse that object, you might as well see what you can do to look.

Sort out shape. Skulless brains. Why not say? Should be an example out of breath.

No thoughts fills out the shape. Wadded batting. Letters to California when I can't get over-stimulated. Feint languishing.

Prurient confidence overrides their barnacles. Rip threatens to eat the plane.

I make what I make through a your it the and retreat to the woods.

And after that and after that I will get all of it being here, there,

METROPOLITAN ENJOYMENT MANUFACTORY
a stressful cannibal

Magnesium wires care and feeding. Dilettante contra profession time-lapse regret passes through backlit horizon. Drawn for quarters.

Need momentary to congruent with present, a slip-case, rubber jumper or bat ellipsis doffs, nothing's good pest and leaves us dragged. Repudiate melanization deference and comfort aspiration when bred is bored, slipping out for a night of frank mask. Rush to get on to the next impress him.

Memorize feelings. Xerox sensation. Contextless ephemera. Grumble, put up with, mock, forget, long for, sample, commit, shed, link, pull the rug out from under, hose, defer.

Mutability gives. Even the worthless character gets talked about. Trade to trust.

Lunge to be seer. Close in on magnetism, the penthouse we play male in. Attach illicit, if you can take, who take care of his person, friend's can't stand getting. Lovers' love a giveaway, stealing busses the children. Let's off steam.

Stainless' pots pickle sleaze more like, adulterated acceptable candy ass'. A few ideas engage, attention books the cad's rivalry. Submission produces submission. Break the extra insert rule—nothing unopposed.

A hairy armpit, one shouldn't, do it again and against, ciphers' giving. Santa love, love contract, love wrong. 1001 shovels' engineer pace is fate. Don't lecture yourself.

Soap rules her. Judge me by consortium. Desire desirability. Pay for attention with looking down from the heights of a tie. Power of powder, best hope, cranks out smiles.

MAKING UP
THINGS TO DO
FOR NO ONE

To guile her illusion.

To generosity chagrin.

To similar stretches in our vices voices.

To wrap ilk-rapt creatures.

To advantage recreation.

To hire all the rage.

To finalize ideal as. . .a reason.

To go on about immorality of connection. (Mixed signals make me affable for a while.)

To give the air a try.

To fly the milk.

To unlucky at both. To get to be what comes along.

To give up because it was all odds. (Live food.)

THE EDGE OF
POSSESSION

I remember what he said to me, I remember what she said to me, I remember what they said, we said; listen. He opened the door to the room that was hot, taking great care that the relics of the saints, cracked and genuine... "Let's get that guy."

I bound him to release me. Will I get to see you? I owned him until they spoke to me. "Thou hast forsaken the sponsor which begot thee, and hast forgotten the executive that created thee." The beast is organization. (Sex sex sex). Entice the subject around his people.

This time he will win, but as the old Chinese proverb says — Chinese Fortune. May your business fail that you will see — profound aversion to reposing in any one view of the world, refusal to be deprived of the stimulus of enigma. (But only indirectly can the landlord pay his rent.)

Now give! How can I make them understand that I am in earnest? They keep sending these priests after me. Doing it for purposes, not to develop a relationship.

Who was her mother that made her no sandwiches, casting off adjectives to carry on? It has to be us. What do you mean give up? I have to get my own.

Rushing requires such attention. (That the channel not slip. (Agent of the moment. Choose the act. Doing it while thinking about it. (Rubbernecking.)))

It is against charity and justice to expose the hidden sin, but not to uncover where the spellbinding instrument is located. (Enticement over time—scale of genre—superimposition, of unmannerliness—crusts of decorative plastics—self-conscious alienation—the possibility that you are not your brother, the zoo keeper.) Give us the energy to be friendly and take her.

Meanwhile the bell was striking all at once. Scratch the bell. (Pebbles all over the ground that describe gravel.) We stand behind our appraisal. There were three of them and one was me.

This sickly portent caused alarm among the ecclesiastics. The senators became priests of the deified superstructure. Without the liberalism that allowed our more radical stances to flourish. . . Now what will we do? Passivity and disenfranchisement, exile, we the demon cast out. How *will* administration treat the lives of the mind? Conclude to suffer? Now will you let me?

Sometimes the show is called belie. We drifted passed the quay, aloof, a partisan. Can you come over to my house Wednesday for some soup? Let Al sit in that window and give us a talk about alluding to it.

Rage backs them off sir, pleats the air. Trepidate to shape the lips. We live hand to mouth.

Many types of cancer may respond to VM-26, because it combines so well with other anti-cancer agents, increasing their effectiveness. His uneasiness of mind was besieged by reproaches from all sides.

Mechanical double, we ought to be doing something about, but I like poetry—creature, of water, in the name of, his response, not to the thing in itself, but to his knowledge of what it was before anything happened, a French beast (Romanum). Is the government revolved?

He tries to guard the tubes of solid state, rule the towels under the door, strengthen across, assaults from the soul evaporate awash in channel four: Moral rectum. Cornbeef square. Leech the museum. We were surprised when we heard the Japanese restaurant was out of sake. Meanwhile the sludge crept toward Omaha.

* * *

Performed when I'm standing here, just a make-believe person cheated the truck. Since we give breaks when serious or urgent, should he need surgery, a private house will be very good for our rendevous. She's still going to be part of your life again.

The best kind of mean, knowing this as a certain person, who wanted to be present at what's more, went to confession before going into the presence of the illegitimate child.

Or is it too late for this decorous conquest. He does not tremble or change the channel. The reason is wanting to die and also show how brave and clarify that grinning face.

These are wonderful qualities in a man and believe me you are very macho. At other times I try to interrupt and sacrifice with ridiculous and indecent sayings . . . if I had only known how to really live. Then remove his foot in the name of Jesus Christ and order him, "Obmustece maligne spiritus."

Just waiting to get his filthy hands on everything that was hers, disputing are you in there. Hello? There are no issues escapes from his tongue and goes to a remote part of the heart and proper into a deep sleep wherein he is shown visions of next week's programming, fantastic visions of what you think you've seen. I assure you you haven't.

Even though it looks like art there will be certain deformities which arise not from an intensity of application, but the second, different and not necessarily better, that leaves him sad and full of confusion.

At this arrival of a good show the old man, filled with fear and disturbed, told the devil to open his mouth so he could fill it with manure.

Sometimes they have no choice, leaving the body in the form of "that's not all she said" and other terrible things. "What in the world has gotten into you?" And the caring will be informed about the needs of all of us in order to receive good-byes and then communicate with musical background music.

With these and other activities advise the victim continuously. Reach into the refrigerator often and very effective. The victim will lose $22.95 and threats. He should derail heart and mind. Those depressed by arrival on the floor may hope for the same. He must be.

After the ignorant and empty threat, joy realizes that spread is giving up and that he is about to leave, because part of our diet to fight cholesterol of the power and order of greasy dirt is really impressed by having a baby.

"I'm sorry, there's a grocery story," that of his companions extinguishing a lighted candle, because some of them are in the habit of staying behind to gloat over their feelings.

Really good, that's nice. They will not be satisfied until they are informed that coffee is bad so we will drink less.

I'm going to look up and down the corridor before the nurse leaves with any luck to go directly to my fault that has been designated by continuing compromises, giving her a project that will use up her time and energy to attend to the clothes and hair of your request for a definite leave of absence. The moment, so lush, so plush, goes out spotty, because I say it can be in different ways, as experience has shown.

That's the eyeopener. I want to avoid that in the form of blazing flame, your permission to leave in the form of wind, bees or ants. Sometimes the official ok is through the ears.

And I plan to go tomorrow, leaving through the heart, stomach and other parts. And I exit from hiding in the shape of a ball. And my feelings for you go through the nostrils, as a restaurant, in drops of blood and in other ways the court will recognize. But you will not believe them.

* * *

Remember what happened until this point. I was trying to say it to you, the candles superimposed on them while they take off their clothes. It used to be my *job* to torment them, but now my happiness is truly complete. So where *are* you? Where in the sense of . . .

You'd better hang onto metal or interior as well as exterior parts. According to your wishes, 'we're here' in both ways. It molds.

This being understood, I wasn't a young girl anymore. The passion never ends. She sings at her wedding. The hit man rambles on at length. The grievance is shipped. (That's why I'm here, to extend it.) Voucher's natural color changes while it isn't here, the phone ring gray or cedar color. Who would ever believe that dirty stuff?

It has something to do with glistening flakes, pinpricks in the pit of the stomach and elsewhere. Those mentioned find out how to use the words they don't dare, gathered here today to turn to spiritual remedies, to show its form, to enter into, to suit him. It's been getting crazier and crazier, and the mattresses and pillows take pot shots at such charms and enchantments, needles, fruit, hair, wax, lead figures.

The feather image of a man with head, hands, legs and arms which left everyone amazed has to be deodorized. Now raisins are a different matter, but are applied in the same manner—gold dust, incense, myrrh, salt, olive, wax and rue—brought to rest by the sin of lust, not in order to feel pleasure, but to garnish her head among the wax fruit.

Resort to I love you, afraid to have your cavities filled in order to have no permanent injury, I swear to you. You're not God; you can't give me any kind of guarantee.

To get you or get you to go, to make use of malice for a wonderful thing, talking to you in the morning, but the opposite opinion is a little brother for continued annoyance. Consecutively you and I undo the new pact for the camera, borrowing from the usurer and that's not all who is exposed of her own accord.

Why police allow some people to be not so sure. I had to tell the truth, the havoc, I feel badly too, for the wrong reasons. I know an awful lot of lawyers wish to enter human bodies and try to obtain such a dwelling place by a knock on the door. I'm not here to exercise visitation rights, nor oppress you with platitudes, but I'm going to touch you or make you go.

Exactly what *do* you know, being reversed and feared through idols and oracles. He cannot reach in. He cannot take revenge against that you don't know anything. I can't see Cliff inditing fantasyland.

She told me you were privy to some semblance. I'll find out believe me I will. It may be an opportunity to save ourselves from the macho, jealous, continental type.

You know that your boyfriend did it, but you want to build a treasury of how you really feel. You deserved that punishment, front row.

I'm going to be the main attraction. Yet another cause may be the sins of the fathers, your dance. To test the faithful, fresh squeezed, have a similar affliction with ulterior motives. The parrot said, "I thought upon the days of old, and had in mind the eternal years."

* * *

In the secular narrative of 'you stay away now' the battle and struggle with every day present themselves. Against the spirits of wickedness in high places . . . for that very reason you apply for the job, recognizing that Adam and Sarah are planning with humility their weaknesses. I can't talk to you privately; I can't have an open discussion with you; come and sit down with a pure conscience. I already told you about that. We had a date, but somebody else came forward.

The unworthy instrument repairs so much damage by making us feel young looking as the afflicted neighbor that with the unique presence of his manner, in some fast company, still being friends, he attributes everything to remembering, draws a salary (motive of esteem), casts out demons, to get to you then in terms we both understand, a terrible liar, did wonders with it, in spite of everything, victims of peace.

Still I think you're right, because I am sinful. Tell him yes, in the hospital, with weapons to prepare and patience, because some of the stubborn and vigilant leave now. Anxiety of separation as nearing closeness stiffens. How lack of confidences leaves you behind with new vigor.

See through the man, per possessionem, and the other. Richard is my husband and he's not here. Frightening shapes find out by experience, with blows, pains of the body, but don't be too long. Whatever you're calling yourself now, I want you to go. Lack of obedience, obstinacy. Let go some of that tension — biting his hands, throwing himself on the ground, in the fire, in the water — take an _____.

Shakes in the presence of trying. (We have to believe that.) Childlike

46

conversation, suggestive movement of the head and hands, the ladder down does not imply rejection, but beginning and entrance.

Mere man takes his place. Hatred of weakness promotes a crank phone call. I really should have your opinion, our mass. Call me if I can help — blaspheming, cursing, abusing, insulting, speaking without having studied the fine points. I know who you are alright.

Arouse suspicion, conjecture, conclude. Sudden change of personality, recurrent nightmares. So quiet because we're prisoners. He tries bribery, he tries approach, he tries to merely say it. Vacate and separate.

Unaccustomed howling and voices, visions, absence of feeling, restlessness, endurance and strength, glossolalia, singing, secrets, can get in, can get out... Talking to her and her face keeps changing and I'm talking in a different voice and then we're somewhere else... Slow pace of realization.

Why? Natural illness, crummy section of town, do you think you could talk to her later? Sounds like he lost his last friend comes up roses.

For his greater glory commit him. Too much despair over losing worldly possessions, familiarity, characterizes this morning. Mother was very secretive. (Flashlight on the rug, guiding.)

Try to learn the way to enter and his method of leaving. Mistreat the body mercilessly in the form of wind, rats, cold water down his back, ants all over the body.

I didn't know I could either. But you know what I can't understand...

* * *

47

A little disorder and irreverence in regard, a picture of the house, so sane, but the stories tell another story.

Ideas are a dime. Perpetrate fraud. Scandalize the people present. Where in the world do you suppose he is hidden?

The how long are you staying in town this time condemns and prohibits it, as my darling too soon, throw me up in a tree, giving them more power than effectiveness, teaches grab her and possess her. (Idle curiosity. (I say the best. (It's for sometimes. (Money burns whole.))))

Don't hesitate to call me. Don't go to the toilet just yet. Don't walk the dog. Don't go to the bank. The sense of being useful of one's neighbor. *It* that matters. How we got to this wording. "I'm going to miss you too sweetheart very much. And if there's ever anything you need, you'll get in touch with me real soon."

Rebuild the sand.

I heard the phone ring twist his tongue, putting the blame on everyone else, and with the first two fingers he never permits sayings or sophistries, but shuts her up with an oath or announcement in her face. So many things all at once in the body of a person, a lot to deal with. The last thing in the world I need.

He doesn't know the meaning of the word, or, a lot of empty conversation put you in this kind of a mood. He may indicate a toe in which the demon should stay until the men handling the search on this end. . . (For his greater torment their names are all signs of proof — tortured serpent, rabid dog or too many people have keys as it is. (Everyone but himself. (At least someone is making a living.))) He reached for the shiny ball.

Resist loving warmth for very long nor learn from him whom he adjures, nor favors, nor credibility, but shallow talk is a sign of close connection, a lot more important than missing dinner, flattery when it comes to something serious, where the spellbinding instrument is located in your accusations, effective immediately. Who *are* his greatest rivals? I have to find a way to get it to get it to go, to learn the meaning of his name, without yoke, abandoned, adversary, beast, fornication, pride, avarice, investigating the stability of lovers.

(We're going to be running into each other again from time to time. (And help us out when you're pregnant, would you . . . never mind.))

Whose pretense has a way with women? Her reasons for wanting to leave threatened our friendship from within and without. What the fuck. Blame him for his only begotten son.

Against the despised give an eye, or replace them by the blade. To shred him raging, quickly give ear to us . . .

We are all standing. This is no excuse. Now that we're alone you can tell me.

She can take an apartment anywhere she can afford it. I'm going to tell her exactly that. Their faces reveal night, acknowledge your existence.

Be gone. I can hold you.

MADE IN CHINA

Panorama: seeping from the upstarts, specimens of hysterics drew exile, corrodes while they banded (personal buckle).

Contrary window—Plane by poles. "Something that would approximate nothing," describes its face, its peer of reprisal for having been born. Sentenced to having been him, playing around containers...

Beautiful like closing the door, eyes either side of their nose, very few doing mostly explaining:

Just clearing things up. I'd like to clear that up, no, I'm just clearing that up. Will you clear that up?

Meanwhile down at bedrock it's no comfortable, not at all. A few people in shoes twelve inches too big, of straw, the shoes, try to plump up a few rocks.

Vinnie ran over Malcolm Bump with a Plymouth. Would he cheat on his wife? Are there scenes! In a quiet upstate way. We go to school; they learn. Instrumental at a distance, while...

Pushing buttons on me I didn't know were there, she left me for slavery. I'd like to bite your lip. We talk about each other, no offense.

How many died; how many were left with a bad taste, but lived on; how many died with a bad taste? Were they respect to their freedom in the tower abut Fisher Body? You gotta. He simply wanted to say no.

Cookie competes, the central concept of emptiness, her reasons for girdle — the giant multinational made no attempt to answer — seed, manifest, perfume.

Closing the door: am I closing the door, should the door ever close; is closing the door closing the door, or, the door is closing to develop (developing closing), when he closed the door he was a _____.

Left to her own devices, her essential working class sympathies developed, but only after years of resentment did they appear as character. They probably want to regard Emptiness as subject, but there is also infinitely cutthroat competition.

We don't want to focus too closely on her occasional impulse to yield to her intuition and had to maintain a closely guarded secret lest her friends at the beauty parlor accuse her of undermining them with her femininity.

Very close to number produced and numbers in operation, for if dreams are images, the tales we fill in might be taken literally or better still conceived with added energy by day. (The gentry families usually required about half the gross produce of their tenants. (We raked the leaves into piles so we could jump into them.))

These efforts sped to wall them off from the impetus that drove them to begin again where neither the rigors of city life nor country isolation would plague them; they tried never to bend to look at them for fear they might freeze into blossom when they ardently wished for change. From among these were chosen the candidates for examination, who more often than not without their clothes could not be distinguished from others of their species.

When she presented six dishes of chocolate pudding to her family of five at dinner, she taught them greed. An elite is enviable.

Who will find room in so little a life. I forgot what they meant by England.

He watered his garden in the rain while wave after wave of Toba, Mongol, Manchu swept off the plains of government spending. Even the vicious dog couldn't imagine a bite of them from the safety of his front yard.

She said she was just reading the package, which taught them the greater wisdom of Paternalism. Pedestrians hold their middles. Good luck to Nostradamus.

In his brown T-Bird he pretended they hadn't seen him. They didn't care who slept with whom, not them. Or even later when it could have made a difference. Everything was so effective on their lawn, as the reason for it—a collusion against the world—sounded less helpful.

Do you think it can still all end in bitterness, despair, sterility? Brown leaves, endless chocolate marshmellows in cut glass bowls, the trigrams of autumn, October 29, 1929, American democracy. When his mat was not straight, Confucius would not sit down on it.

She phoned to assure separation was proper and orderly. Japanese rock garden. She should have known better. When the government of empire is done along with farming, we must make our play and secure our position simultaneously, when the iron is halt.

So one night she took out her luger and shot him as he slept, and then she shot herself.

Precise mathematical reasoning, he had had enough success by age 17 to feel its economic surplus until by wind, friends dead or despised, no more beautifully conceived luncheons, buffet suppers among the blighted elms.

Left is not contained in two, plus if you come right out he gives you encouragement. The know how to kiss while mixing martini.

About five minutes now, the Chinese mind asserted itself in Zen and piecework, we laughed at the few cases allowed, but clearly we come to qualifying for jobs other cheerleaders could not cope with. They needed too much aspirin to be much use.

The contrast between the two schools is much deeper, across the Hudson Valley and beyond to the Catskills where they all would sleep to avoid such pressure. But as we made you in the back seat, you complained of a sunburn.

The dog and his bone relish waiting, for the tv subtext, from which this protégé of ambivalence, for the front and sides of your face, as he lay his curly head upon his pillow, "If I caught my death, I'd put him in a jar and feed him every day."

Like the wrench, nine sense, he ought to know. Every family has a book. Derange a trois: treat with wondering drugs. Putting wheels on the Americans.

The world too us and left pawing around among stones with half smiles. I stopped with my trained dog act. The monkey is not a dope. Not represented by any one person, Spencer Tracy. Jack slept whenever he wanted and when he awoke, he'd bathe his war wound and come into the kitchen and say, "Got anything to eat, Ma?"

Nice tract to develop, thought Candaules.

And when you're making it, you don't have to forget. You don't disappear then and you don't have to finish it up with a flourish. You don't have to make it perfect. It's not like you're going to make some big speech of something in front of the Shriners, you. You, you. You you you.

Sheet over the face signifies. . . Hug a, I just wanted someone to play with. Since you've been gone, my bathtub won't fill up.

Flowers are higher than homework in the hierarchy. I pass, I subsidize, I rake the hoe, also, I forgive the hothouse, to cultivate oneself to give security and peach. And many was the time she repeated in her plot with him that no housewife floozy ever farts like the whoppers that shook from her rosy red can.

Shape the minds, stay green and understand the working principles: association through categories. Ravages both faces no matter how they seek to hide their. . . subsidizes into the ground.

Shape the minds, stay green and understand the working principles: association through categories. Ravages both faces no matter how they seek to hide their. . . subsidizes into the ground.

And yet the offended parties insisted that uprightness did not signify severity or justice, but rather impartiality, guidance from accepted principles instead of personal preference.

(I especially like natural art, but really understand how certain more neurotic types need formal stimulation, plastic surgery, 10% debentures, unilamellar vesicles, all that periphery that the city of the mind allows for its decoration, because as the Darwinian principle operates by change among the least fit, so when times are good there is a greater proportion among those fringes to afford change, disorientation, apathy, haunt the shopping centers and whistlestops trying on gloves.)

The White Picket Fence (the bull with his horns caught in it (in educaton there should be no class distinction (in words all that matters is to express the meaning))). I love my husband and children.

In the whiteness of her whites she crossed the court. With a little money begin to be very happy. Where the lines are out of bounds. A way of living not a living which confuses. At love / forty she stopped serving.

A tennis pro, a commercialized vehicle of togetherness, rape among the servant class, an aging luxury automobile, structuralist rhetoric, prix fixe, misery of hunger, your serve, anxiously awaited rendevous, he married his secretary and divorced his wife of the house and kids. If I were dead, it would solve everything.

Earnestness, liberality, truthfulness, diligence, generosity not far from the city but with plenty of green around, field stone renovated circular drive, play room, extra good. My young friends, why not study to get ahead.

The 7:40 pulls out of the station. In the book it says, "Life is boring, but if I inject myself into it, it will become vital." Is the book well thumbed? Is every simple statement a reification? If we like words, are there not solutions we can agree to? Jasmine, Amber, S?

Sofa stranger, percentile writing, sex reflex. Polite impossibility of faith.

Not by chance alone do they do. Towaway. For a purpose ((((((((as in organized for a meaning. The inner city reaches our. . . I don't know when I first conceived of the plan, but I carried on with a certainty of having had ulterior motive from the first.

We would be free by discipline, but he kept singing the blues, "Gonna get down, Momma, on that second person, you." Until I was blue and he. And for all his words on the subject. A sense filters out of. Gone to further.

We kept going, dragging each other. Not why should I protect him. I dragged him through while he hummed "Cocktails for Two" and considered it a sign of superior being. As if by saying not this not that, he would make what he did not understand or care to understand irrelevant, leaving him on top of a pile of shit instead of in the middle of it. The basis of the intelligent approach to life. Gone to further.

And yet I will not say how I was perfect. Gone to further.

Some stay to, some say. There is no such thing, she divined, as perfect attitude. Pedant businessmen swarm the links while foreign nations plan revenge.

To weld the classes as if by acceptance, disintegrating their symbols of hatred and fear into tools, then making those into themselves, not violas of the music but a musical hammer.

Those who work hard and still do not learn. A changed view of men includes women, but is sex as a way of number.

To undermine fashion as much as tradition: individuals as a measure of happiness except me doing what I want because I thought of it.

So much time to do so little. Business goes from bad to worse. Your death, would profit me.

Let's get busy without work and chat later. The stupid and intelligent do not change.

I'd like to come down out of the air. "I am always astonished to hear the name of a bird I hadn't known." I feel alternately. . . . I am reached passed poetry.

A lush lawn can mean a full septic tank. I am hurt if you don't recognize me.

The inferior man scratches his itch: Interpretive, philosophical and often subjective, the managerial panel determined in favor of loyalty to workers. Although he denied group prejudice, he often spoke of we. It or that principle or paranoid. The panel voted to admit colored interpretations.

One is not a tool. It is not a tool. Not for or against. Stop making decisions. One thread, many sides, mixed metaphors. If you want to make a killing, you must invest. If the golden rule is beyond me, a changed altitude becomes inevitable.

The color of her cheek. The nothing short of dramatic. Let us live in houses of steel and glass, since they will not easily decay. I miss you when you go.

Everyone has standards and even I may have some attributed... Grimy safety.

Scratch the surface of the problem. "Jobs are for profit." Even politicians behave more liberally and selflessly than artists, which is not a point on the scale of either.

As the cities decayed those middle class families who could not afford the Yellow River moved beyond the limits of the Golden Horde to where they could live near the excitement, but breathe the cleaner air of the environs.... Association (Art does not come from making images, sic, Charlton Heston as Moses.)

You know what's going to happen, but you have to go through it and it keeps going on and on. Due to the baby sitter.

Direct motoring and combinations of train riding enabled moves within a 50 mile radius of their workplace to the result that of a few decades some in the most populous and developed parts in the country were transformed to vast areas where continuous urban and quasi-urban settlement.

We wish Momma would come home, I feel very depressed, because I cannot get a grip on what my life, living in filth and degradation under the aegis of living like an upright and moral man, a philosopher, a sage among the beautifully. . .

Making Chinese slaves into serfs increased profit and making the serfs into freeholders a way to increase profit. She called her lover agriculture of hair.

Tolerable understanding, absorbing the character of the people to put him endearing to earning a living.

High chair, Sally the baby, mirror, corner, Cape Canaveral, cumulus, intelligent but not creative, you can do anything but what you do best, besides I have no summer clothes, I would like to feel better, corrected and published with love and kisses for all.

I idealize all my friends' lawns. I am self-absorbed as an actress. Generosity/success. (Hurt Bunk) Limey, Inc., a shoplifting cooperative.

We two being then old may finally understand each other. His enemy from a former life became his son-in-law whose career he was forced to advance in order to secure wealth for his daughter. After that they all lived in harmony. Regular sex and no constipation. They worked hard cleaning the yard, although the children did not want to do their share.

Never be guided by arbitrary law, which has great influence with ignoramuses who pretend to be clever. Hollow theories for purposes.

A difficult task we have ahead to dispel when the trials for which we have been trained in humanism are set before us.

If you are not ashamed, no one will shame you. I cannot decide what to eat and the bill of fare only confuses me. Great training of gentry society enabled them to rule the empire. Consider the substance of her plea not her breasts or moans. I can sign my name very well.

So positioned that he can't imagine currency beyond his own ideas. Writing is not therapy.

A dead running to sell victory by jingo to the forest.

Is agony necessarily beatific? Do rituals come last? He took his face out of the sink. Art is development.

She wrapped every sandwich individually, but by lunchtime they had all leaked into the ting. A pattern to the whole. Basis of moral order. Her tongue in my ear (t / e contact). They drove her parents' car over the muddy football field.

Herman, vomit on the lady. Although bamboo painting was no mean achievement, it served the same purpose as plain or lacquered panels.

Lifelike stone, structure through much work, of language, appropriation, composition, numbering pages. All six are excellent special, persons we love to be with and who have a lot to offer, beyond the baseline. Canon.

Shopping lists: down the aisle. There is no end to naming them without elaboration.

The form of phone calls, tone and atmosphere, putting the forgotten, atmosphere of living rooms decorated in a single color, vital tone or atmosphere, manipulate for another reason. They like to show up the words, but tone and atmosphere rather than verisimilitude.

Second grade sex, quaintness, how we tried to be, assembling people together like Chinese characters implies a new meaning, words do.

Suddenly I understand how it all works and possible to fix, and I want to puke.

His cunt, glossalalia, shutter pulse, and inside the door was a switch on the right, *Not Necessary* with Fred Astaire. OK boys, the Americans are gone, get back to work, this ain't no picnic, we got a job to do, delivering the milk, subsection to pause.

Cellular Catholicism, listening for the mistake, the little angels, look down through the bannister, I was small and wanted my measles, one of us was dust, aspect, eloquent money, the was, the sure was, divisive know, not too much, drain scuppers, esses of the bonefish rag.

Two of us was enough. Epistle crux. Now every work is Monday in justification for the poet's proclivity of administration, drunk with wine, the squinty eyed guy, standing in front of the post office in Windsor, Vt.

"Don't Let Me Stray" in chalk in front of his 8a social studies class before they fired him for subversion.

A dead running. Ten foot hills, one foot trees, one inch horses, and tenth of an inch men, half seen like eyebrows. There are certain formulas. The lower part of hills are blocked off by streams, pathways are blocked off by men and women strolling at their leisure.

He stood behind the baseline and his powerful ground stroke carried the ball into the next. . . .

C H ' E E ' P E   D ' I R R ' I T

1.

I ha' gibbon itout t'you ther on th'kvetch, I ha'gibbon itout t'be done; e then itis gibbon e sd. E what ha' ben done? Must I comout ther e shake ebryone'v you by yr. personalized modules? Geton w / it b'for you ha'to see me, b'cause that will be worse than what you ha' t'do.

He had been french-fenced for two seeks and felt a bit like lunch meat, olive loaf perhaps, if history served him right, or Rostov-steffian views of Mars to break out of fortune, deathly afraid that whose-will-is-it would squelch the wrecks he'd reconnoitered from steroid miasma. Upshot? The girders, New Jersey rocket pockets, no sense to maintenance seemed like freedom. Hoping to wake up and find out it wasn't him and it wasn't him, it was them who made him feel it and it was him feeling it, not that philosophy offered more than a song until what appears disjunct exposes how to talk about it.

Given an intro, sprockets began to unwind beside his ear. She told him with her eyes that it would be true which was why he deferred until he found out it had come true. That was when he started to actually, just before it took his head off.

So if the sea is on that side, it must be Rio, eh? How you know it's not a lake, and if it's on the other side, it's Santiago? And then what if we turn the tv around, it's Dakar? Separating the ones that did not know from the end of the deli system from it's a matter of a hunch today or a scatter. (There's got to be logic.) Great combo art and

61

money, and yet persist imagining I saw her and that was that. The passengers' fine leather strap frayed despite net increases.

The elevator described it up to the 95th floor and malfunctioned through the roof as she had feared, arcing over police with anticipating dogs. Fortunately Ace had his pod on tight, his mark in the float marts on V-V, and before abstraction could climb out, escape and leaped, landing his marsupial on the ball of a flagpole that carried the Association's banner in another age. But as he slid down, the vitriolic grime, accumulated from hunger, disintegrated the sheath, leaving him baked by the time he reached safe dirt.

This was no time to mend his stays. He had attributed direction to his descent and losing partners from eroticism was not his idea of proper coercion, but he grabbed brass anyway. The tarnish left a tingle of victory on his hands.

Yelling at space inspired optimism. He wanted out. He gave the ruse its due. But all the options seemed more risky than bed vacation, so he took it for a weak narrative instead of what it might itself be. Another of his inventions conned the cadet into lunch passes. He had not the courage himself. There is no end to generalities, the safety of spheres, all the wants all clean.

2.

When the monolithic propulsion mentality entered the hydrogen kitch atmosphere of a failure, its starved motivation drank deeply and renewed, flushed back toward that from which it had eons ago sailed, picking up planets, destroying, perfecting, linking, drawing power until, the central pretense, atom and particle conglomerating around the solider self at the core, compacting even trash until, critical mass achieved, emanated across the spectrum of every radiation down to a schmuck. Then he phoned.

What was coming out? Of callow, why not? Of the self he would never go to the movies. Of spit he quivered, which had driven him in in the first place. It was too pointed a detox to rest easy on. The solutions was a couple of details ago, but he couldn't remember. It continued, however, to be him.

It thus when the ball sound sucked each other through a field of whifty ribbons, flabby torture separates no one from no one and who is left who cares anyway from what they're taught to do to each other, so I taught her was all attention required. "Teach me things," she could say that, and I supplied the willing slaves of Mullet she belonged to berate in her next defamation. It was the perfect ploy to get there, but where would it get me, but would I have the jot to go, just go, if you know what I please, and there it would be left again, along, left, primitive, with a black method of useless jolts, lorrying along the journalists ply of reassurance and provocation.

Thus is a country run by old men and on atmosphere. They sprung from farms, wiped turds with leaves. The aliens were disgusted and fooled, chasing bellybutton lint through realms of illuminated periods. They fell upon each other at last despite intimate recognition both intuited, but. . .must.

Yet this is called piece and freedom, a 2 am attach where even the cat is jarred out of napping. Even the hosannahs of predilection are signing a shower of vanity to the hunter and plowman, streaking across an auditorium where nothing but the last mum of the blast echoes from which to reconstruct.

To impose penumbra, sowing tandem cudgels above that spinal disturbance, give me some now; not sorry, no, not, thought another painted city of noses whose profiles press against galling and blond.

3.

Perfect disingenuous tone while all shattered incisor, lecture on the merits of gas, transforming the race by clinging to opinion, impolite and phosphorescent personality attributed by other authors' lack of cunning that's rotting clone. Fill'er up very friendly. Inserting a tube in each of her ears, he switched on the blinking machine.

Qwerty swallowed at the ship as it geared into hyperspice and carried along by its dementia found himself alone once again with his thick legs and arms, narrow chest denoting heavy gravity and abundant oxygen, if you call what you do there breathing. The bones of a 16 billion year old bone of a ship on an asteroid growing one rock about one o'clock, a time to fiction one's feeling, participate in abundance and let it get out of hand, less righteous than many pills are willing to let them limit to, because they want to end it, tie down the rigging and other pretexts from laziness.

Reasoning all out for you, separate geography of ice, creatures you imagine will appear loving — the cat a friendly bull, the word nursery rhymes — or find out Padwaks kept thinking he was alright, accidents just kept happening all around him. The toy bridge projected into a test tube universe that allowed inhabitants to boot an erg from home base.

"Butt th'beggar out, Little Sister." "I get that got," in her penchant for corners. "Quaff his Nero, if he gots no." "What shill do chip?" "Sift around nut purity; help is in your way." "Beat me with real estate." "Simis doesn't live here anymore, if you call it that, Htrer."

Bag for it. Left handle. Enamoured of quality, because of the credulity with which the citation system salutes and more especially, because it was something undefinable and hence more valuable like the Holy Spirit excites awe that love of the Son and authority of the Father can never perspire, he would allow fellows to walk on him to inspect them from underneath and lost whatever value was consigned to the rubbish heap by hive-minded squirts, but not even this perfect, his perception of personnel hired to footprint his chest, since secret knowledge unaccessed, that it had not use to the world, and hence the world overlooked him as he himself, striving to get out of this morass by self-knowledge; to what end. He made one up to cherish with sidereal vanity, perceptions gathered, as it were, reaped from the hysteria of his involvement. The mouth of the engineer trainee.

Bring the bag in. Is what is. Hang from her solid middle that generations from never to overcome except by intimation, smeared on and incapacitating them, the responsibility trapline laid all the way back to desperation, were trace value instead of their own—the twisted cause of writing how it is being writ. If other than injustice, we'd say something—asparagus, beautiful scenery in bad movies, love for a friend appearing weak to him, emerging personality as story. So get to be Noone.

Chugging through the tenement of stars, the freighter's occupants, unaware how instrumental they would be in another frame, what writing as critique must interchange with what he's really trying to do—reconstitute the body in the form of words, like orange juice, but the question so the question why didn't he just take fresh squeezed (but friction rot on narrative thrusters, first so bright, so soon gone immortal, gone, immortal. The engines flared, *, then ,) in the machined part of his justified modesty in the service of space travel given over to received ideas; yes, you can think it out, but a way out? Dents where forehead was. The great debt of words to farts.

4.

It seemed he pine that Fwap could hold he own against them if he didn't have to worry about anyone's pelf, but up's and down's were still he problem. The moment he back was turned the kind of space-out he had been used to—critical sass—let he person coagulate in front, he behind still he statistic. Large nervous hands. Nonsense leaving he planet when he machine can.

Clientele landscape in the sun of evening she reined in her mount. The frozen countenance of image, intersecting levels of animate life and meaning, directs the previous period for which nostalgia for who we think we are plumps up a pillow to ignore the context of a gesture, which regaled her in trapezoid, which seems brutal when so isolated, but in its place rates merely a release from stress like the demise of a planet one can reason out too well. Matriarchal propaganda convince them they share. The real thing, so much to go for.

That take time, node / cower, forget by then inadequacies of beginning, how it didn't get the point to speak so fast, content to suffer or to speak to effect, but by wearing stretches, loosens, falls around the ankles and there you are anyway who had not so tried to point.

And now you know what you want and get it by astrology. Making by being made, composition by contusion, here the pail handles, palisade, commerce of dugs among pilotry, the magnesium shells not teachers, priests, shrinks, 'imaginative' type, psychoids, parsley heads from tragedies, android tree lice, in fact you your eyes only. His arm was a little loose, fuck you connectors having stretched, smug pivots on its climber.

Norchem loped through purple and yellow balloon vibes with a pinto. He needed extra stimulation techoids to transmit compunction that far across the room to share. The bomb-phones rattled the solar twinkie. Purchase on reflection by his thorns.

Insist on being swallowed. But is looking that? Crinkling if there's one revert, she said his name as if trying to convince us he was really alright, assured gravity, as the riven fled the she, all details washed off the map by unexpected good weather that lets grumpiness show.

Concession: The unusual nouns of imagination change nothing. Still you want to question 25-foot vegetables with hard grey outer skins and green feeder antennae beginning where stalks multiply. Simple, it's connectors.

Need protection social natural variation. Smell. Leer. Moral tone of ideation. Protective sarcasm. And. Smokey. Final. Or. And. Thus. And / or. Max or min.

5.

Trying to make what Rywith said come true, the gull foots down the ice. Trying to make it so convincing like him or authoritative as a dream. Go on making it. She was on Mike and he asked her, you know what she said? So trying to live up to it. The mothball fleet comes to live with in-laws, saving the day. The teacher's loud voice and overdeveloped organs of generation.

Make decisions about the universe to participate. Get kicked in the head to be able to cry, standing up to institutions. Call up her vices; the symptoms were chosen. How deep and personal to get your truth? Making man and woman equally forceful is a guardian. Easy access. Suicidal sex drive forcefield. If everything is understood. The world is what is — yellow, green and black buildings, oppressed trees man the transit shop.

Less mantle over Wall St., maximize potential of Florida turtles. Relaxing or vacationing on index cards. Extrapolate by doing a lot of technically perfect, irrelevant wringing of the hands. Keep worth up you. The little house that reads palaver with blue and yellow wood-work by the boat yard within which blink six yards of lights and an ominous but friendly inhabitant. Putting all the sources together then, how sorry will you be to not have your ears washed.

Get there just in time to get it fixed. The big butted nurse wants a home to fix. There is no end to self possession. Give all out, not all away. Sultry hammock. Explaining snow. Creosote wraps. Muddying waters. Geriatric textures. How we love the giant entity holding a knife to our throats. Fixed disintegrates or built up. The words analyze your ear wax to a vitriol, extrapolation from what is, morals in case social structure begins to crack, but not otherwise, mutating until you get to it, didactic edge of impersonal forces. Pop music is the great political tool.

What you know girl, no use railing at Abe, unless you gonna breakfast. Fascination trajectory. Bobbing for reflection. Simper fricassee.

New woman. Getting as much as you want out of speculative reasoning. (Why they always deride it.) Old woman reorganized. The same woman later. A woman decomposed into atoms for teleportation. Alien woman's cleavages. A woman you know or like to know. The right to be your own boss: ten tripes that signal he is or close to it. A woman you don't want to know, but. Another woman.

6.

Happiness gene. Fusillade of creatures as through a Fragonard. Insufferable nasal passages crave acid rain. The best of both worlds. Preventative nova. To read for the sensation of moving your eyes moving the other organs. Imagination transplant. Cuspidor synergy. Entropy is the end of entropy.

Still less for applied philosophy. There isn't enough consensus. You can tell from the outside. What they realized about the canals of Mars was that they would do anything one asked. Absorbed by professionalism. Terrible throughout the tenure of her breath. Early industrialization group. Summer is ready, sir. Nuclear mish mash. A darling Yugoslav among the stars.

There's only the other side of our world. You moult the outer nervous sentry delude. I press the button on your flank for lunch. Not until you know me better. The little rocks in my shoe. Stealing is on the way out in our galaxy, because since the advent of the Authoritarian body, everything has become uniform. Extent of abandon. If the earth were flat and infinite, the sun would be new every day. They were nervous enough to be obnoxious to listen to — no sympathy for their burnt vanes. Consolations of state take over. Use my type as well as intellect to get the monitor position. Industrial sag.

Psychology of space travel. The string bean rocks. The landscape and weather of diodes. Hard science really of pencil erasers devoted to an increasingly locked up notion of society as a house.

Wandering on the face of it, in order to go back in, freedom as expansion, up to his neck in a hairy hill, go out and start your own universe. Zero civil. To actually evaluate that a perfect facade indicates internal decay. Literalness of new physics ambiguity.

"Are you free to deposit some in here?" she pestered the striped bugs. Hard to know how the drama of their system reached us, minds groping a window on our world, producing concern that we were about to be revealed. Nice as a drone. Would Irew be free for about 20 minutes; we just want to run some tests on her.

A fracture freer or less so, fewer strung out individuals, the heroic cutting edge, freeing oneself from machines, new feudalism, on a regular world or one with noticeable weather — ice, fire, sand, water, air, vegetation, animal life. Dr. Cobra did not play William Tell with his wife, simply self-aggrandizing, earth-bound sadness, under the earth fear, heavy metal solar system, junk food asteroids, hyperorganized galactic sectors, 1,000,000,000,000,000 unique worlds in different colors. Forces of deep space. Bugs of time, machine minds. Dimension of change. Quest, conquest. Small part of a big picture. An idea over millennia.

69

PLUS THIRTEEN

1. Usefulness
   a. Interlocking zones of varied configurations
   b. Colorful tools
   c. Precision of ambiguity
   d. Corral with the gate open
   e. Nourishment

2. Anti-entropic Forces
   a. Perception of subtle differences
   b. Events consistent with common experience that appear as unusual occurrences
   c. Shape determining use
   d. Commitment
   e. Lazy arts

3. Presence
   a. Details reinforcing axioms that vary with those details
   b. There are more ghosts around in the daytime
   c. Inclusion of self as one of the materials
   d. Mental processes interlock at the right moment to say
   e. Synthesis / Fusion, i.e., control

4. Accessibility
   a. Xanadu
   b. The door out of the church
   c. Toward the politics of language
   d. Her swimming pool filled
   e. A woman undressing behind a bead curtain

5. Approach
    a. Fullness recognized as
    b. The seat belt sign lights
    c. Cutting the Gordian knot
    d. Errors are volitional and the portals of discovery
    e. Early dawn mountain time with surface fog

6. Inertia
    a. Slipstreaming
    b. I was just passing on my way to
    c. An unusually wet spring
    d. Chick hopping about on a frying pan
    e. Nothing suits me like my union suit vs. monumental cottage industry

7. Fruitfulness
    a. A fable or skepticism
    b. Values inhere in forms
    c. Prime numbers
    d. Calculus: solution to paradox
    e. Holidays

8. Ways of Seeing
    a. The two hole experiment
    b. Recognition of limitation
    c. A fog descends or lifts
    d. Cathexis
    e. Rbt. Smithson also ate, slept, fucked, went to the movies, etc.

9. Motion
    a. Within stillness
    b. Artesian well
    c. Ideas in things
    d. Calligraphy
    e. Perpetual motion (rebirth of Jerusalem)

10. Discontinuous Functions
    a. Perceived time
    b. Hierarchy of concerns that changes with each application
    c. Small differences in lovers' breathing
    d. Conversation with a friend
    e. Refusal of something to be categorized

11. Linkages
    a. Waiting until a minute passes
    b. Today's bath
    c. The many single paths on the trail to Mecca
    d. Right hand to right hand or right hand to left hand
    e. Consequences of truth

12. Remembrance
    a. Daze
    b. A wooden house sheltered among conifers
    c. The artist's studio table
    d. Walking up stairs
    e. Forgetfulness

13. Additional Configurations
    a. Encyclopedia
    b. A 'Polaroid'
    c. Both
    d. Attentiveness
    e. Additions

PLUS THIRTEEN

1.

The playyard faded into woody hills, a boneyard of efficacy for the electorate, reviving unspoken thoughts as spur, visible through layers of varying viscosities that purport through pepsied generations to conform to present day forcefulness of personality when confronted by an onrushing car. Include you in the partnership. Shapes of heads in Egyptian sculptures lip to lip with those on American coins, or, my skull is no help for its hair. Distances between thoughts and the propositions they engender lay out front, I mean, I can say it for included, for the book train, for turn tattoos and forget to develop something more — three paces north, two steps south, and to turn the epileptic in step with cordials and cantilevered appliances is accomplished with five expatriates.

The raised lettering on the cover of the novel lies under the glass ashtray which overflows with half-smoked Vantage butts. Ditty blocks. If only I could be satisfied philosophizing about my childhood. Silver corkscrew. Prayerrug. Rusting farm machinery from the late '40's when I feel like dinner in summer. Among the cathedral pines, inside the lean-to a charred stick the point of which through stirring had been scoured down to unburned oak. Ma Bell's ear, the design firm letterhead, Mott south of Canal, Vegas nights and pressure ridges chime the pottery lambs in the breakfront, attracting, for the sadness of congruence, their hue of the 100% paper paper that the female spy's wine glass, the coat you found in the trash, Mediterranean cities, "a rose red city", *Cities of the Red Night*, Marineland of Disneyland, my dictionary of the walnut desk, your hair on the sill, L.A. freeway choices in the year the chocolate syrup flowed unevenly over the short-stack, contracts stacked neatly among golf tees, more attention the longer they last.

You know what you done. It in the it which within which it's that. I question your question because it makes me claustrophobic. So orderly no one would stay. "We don't need those stacks of bricks anymore." What the president is thinking. Not dreaming. There *are* factories out there. Mr. Dreyfus feels weird in the following sense. . . . Venus of Sunset. Sense of the sentence(s). Breathing through the mouth. You can't run a sales campaign on golf. Milquetoast resurgence. Give them a minute and they break. Gift horse of the mouth. Superbus subjectivus. Recalcitrant hobos. Giving up with the Joneses. Several weeks after I want her, as opposed to the red laceless shoe or his paranoiac pregnancy, rather drenched Madras, whose story of your padded belly and nippleless breasts of mammoth proportions took the boys' breath in. Critical examples throughout. An underlying story then? A kind of vocabulary. Layered kinds of Lesbian separatist supremacy, to become independent, counter change. Poetry *and* science, a turn of the hands of the aisle. Clear about alienation and about what he means. Can you think the pinball around? Repercussions when you think about frivolity of the ditch. She felt him become her bye, the word word-pair. Passing through nadir, adjectives are the other. Overcome literalness or allow literalness. Writing black or white.

Principles of alternation. The deer streaks passed the tiger. Clause. Sense of direction taking. Not having to watch the keys. Subject not subjectivity. The elements that identify a space placed in which shine establishes surface and dimensionality. . . Her breast of mourning. Possible grammars: of speech, of syntax, of narrative, of whispers, of machines yet to be blueprinted; Darwinian hunting. He said we could move out anytime we wanted. If you buy this, we'll give you another one free. (The words that makes open.) Her phone. What is that? Recognition of presuppositions affecting precognition. Although she had a boyfriend, she said she'd keep the gate open for a more propitious moment. Anger moral surplus. No exceptional concessions have been allowed. Faithfulness. Faithlessness, conventional courtesy. Taste for discrimination. Principles without politics. Give yourself out of purity. I know you don't want something meaningless, but I make meaning. He gave me to speak. I.U. escape. He noticed his predictability in their boots. Pushing through foliage of assaults. Divorce makes many more couples possible. Vagueness of first stammerings. Radical questioning of the foundations is a kind of irony. Rule confused with certainty, meticulousness with rigor. . .ah, dispiriting formalism. Why we lived together was lost and the atmosphere in the room became more and opaque. I her personal camouflages, wheel reticent to opacity.

"Contract" "contrac" 'contra' contr' cont. con eyrie. Raconte Racoon found an alternative. Do not close the gap with words. Has made her man. "Public life subject to the laws of urinary segregation was the first sign that local government, a closed system made of a large but limited family, supreme in its power and ubiquity, but extending no further than encroaching, had given way to a larger governmental unit, no further up to the level of the unit immediately superior to the sentence.

Mouthe contents. And choices — this / that vital part missed by the bullets that couldn't kill. Health food as medicine doesn't threaten Lutece. Happy turtle owners. Welfare triptych. Local magnifies. Tiger solution. I gave Michael the bum's work to modestly print. Roots Beauty Salon. Terraced woodgrain. Masseter. Swimmer. Indicate obviously. Straighten survival. You're not crazy *enough*. Aware is phonability. Contact is activate spell it out. Vanilla cone BMW. Not a sandwich, alternation. Flagellum of obvious example. Alarm clock corner. Crudity. Although I'd known him many years, not much had transpired between us, but I had his address, a furnished room in an ex-foster home where he bared his arms on his nourished knee. Fear monk of the hand's estate. Glove making, that which the wall on a clove or two with the top down by perpetual maintenance ground up reason on a note corresponding to the key pressed. Progressive. Foundation of the Tower of Babel.

2.

Perception of subtle differences. Cold we hear and spell. Optimum security: to be not there. Sad boys can't tell the differences. I mean, defeat depart disembody. Hear here. As a whistle, tongue rolled back, the wave rolls over art, adorning it, hearing you cry. This / series of us being here, but with differences so I can't tell what happened, we stopped giving a chance and agreed to pop me that mass happiness; but why. We worked out rules to understand and all you understand is that you don't care to. We have meant it to glance sidelong to where your waist is on your body. Each of your phone numbers signifies, in its last four digits, a quality you have relating to the atmosphere of the year it reads. 1920. 1082. 1538. 1958. 7911. I hear you saying that. It happened in such a way that I could not grasp it, though I knew it had happened. Egoism. Egotism. Egoist. He go east, burned by the bride. Will you let pigs build buildings out of bricks? (Each an egg of ingress.) The pupils of the brown eyed man. Frilly Fillet: A complete work on each subject. Happenstance afloat. Consequently continent. Elegies—a kind of dairy product. The heft of the lift (list(typed)). And, but, to, etc. A subject everything we say after a while, is an effort; defeat whittling. Very good for thinking, but very good for drinking. Gaudy generalities of aphorism aside, each of us had a nose. Maybe just me wants more, built models every day, to make more sense. Narrative.

Chewing his fleas, he paces off circumstance to indicate where the neck is recombinent. I ordinarily would be *there* Sunday, with frogs in the drawing room, thousands of feet on the same stare, blinking the ache of commune and looking awkward. Cans of beans on supermarket shelves play too much thinking to make italic notice where her skull beneath blond skin, counter remedy, peels off, acquiring habits to be useful later. In the drive-in for instance or in public baths that new car smell forecasts weather for next year, Indian's corns nailed to the wall, pussy willows wickered out with good. No end to possibilities of each but the other, how singular one is, saying he is not a crook. Lift the greed lamp, man, like the verb that gave us more chance than the be together allotment. Slipping the porch pooch antifreeze, kinda small, but he sang, "Vegetarian Thanksgiving Henna," paper candy, brain turkey, sanguinary, outsize desires suppressed & alphabetized in the catalog, the whole family sounds alike but acts differently, not to mention whatever standard they post over the lintel. Eyeball to eyeball, everyday butterfly pinned to newsprint, cathechists wait on wafers for the laugh not suppressed on the train. Pressure releases the game to sequester more Daniel Boone sausage, the delta drawing them out of the breaks and mudflats thinned out by sheer nights. I got a lapel ready. Go home. Agreements breeds. . . . Friendly threats argue for wars. Why not a fourteen year old to repeat one's surprise. Hyphenated, Fats Domino talks girl talk waiting for starving child prostitutes, a game that constantly changes rules, dingy squeezing through the walls. Scene changes necessitate praise of shoes, right words, lucky to escape, the ballad of certain conclusions. Go out feeling left, perfect harmony. The cambium has succeeded in the hollow center. The lost maple leaves glue and he hunkers for your passport, an interim skull outlawed by other curators. What was happening to him finally overcame his will and he could see he was seated on a marble bench nestled in ferns while beyond burned the fires of an extensive garbage dump. An event here is it. Overdramatized conversational gestures betray graphic arts suppliers in principal cities.

"And so I used to jerk my limbs about and make various noises by way of indicating what I wanted, using the limited forms of communication which were within my capacity and which, indeed, were not very like the real thing." Her body gave one the feeling that obvious for grotesquely perfect solitude. How hard you have to work to shape the mean as necessity, the fringes shape it—the match, the doughnut, the tunnel diode (where you see it and when you don't. (genre of poetry)). . . . Their exemplary lives, her inspiration. He grimaced in pain on the commuter train, then went back to reading his newspaper. Curing our respiratory ailments with homeopathic remedies, lest we snort it all, sewage treatment plant sculpture, aerodynamic frogs and turtles, sonnets as filler, palisades at Greystone. He took her 'preposition' the English Garden. How to notice. The building I'd like to live in. She slid off the saddle into the bath. He wanted to charge the poorly dressed girl 95¢, but when she produced $2, he asked for 90¢. Relaxable river. Panic barge. Right then she had so relaxed him that he almost. She wanted to have a place where people could go, proselytizing to make me feel better. The hands of men and women, stable sculpture, destabilized constructs. Reggie's pancreas. Putting a phrase in this to let you. Pattern and form of the existence which they had . . . . pattern and degree of existence.

Sign. Turned out a lot, that none of them did it. Mr. Pines turned his back on the contract. Going into it at length, pruning Justice Department cuticles. Once begun along the path, the possibility of error haunted him less, but he tired of it long enough to rest on a single subject that they could follow. Adherents. (Put in formula for adhesive.) When it was time to split, however, there seemed to be no alternative other than give up the parking place. Shakes until the tram arrives, one track branches, tells, as the symphony coal crane looped, alliances into the drink. Like to remember how it was shying. Easy Access Inn, Inc. When the maestro raised his baton, the Church lost the merit of belief: He's a good employee, but doesn't like to be crossed. So complicated no one would read it, organized only by content, Barry, given importance. Chance to write this down while gulls bob for trash. While the angel is telling her this she's looking at her shoe, thinking how frayed. Near the water or near the store. As he let go of the hammer, he blew. Doubtless that was all Frish wanted and he got it and then meltdown began — justification for infinite restless desire. To lemma a story line in possibilities of four types. Word, pair, sentence or phrase, linked sentences and phrases of varying commitments to grammar. Mispelling it, even for increased awareness of intention, second spellings, might cause Barbara's letter to be given less credibility. You have had the chance to explore subtler sentiments. Imitating poetry. The clearest he said it. Asking often shows enough interest. Choice of pop culture figures to admire, given the choice part. Kicking the old black woman out of her seat, to fix the mechanism beneath it. Every year he extended his field, but since World War II a tendency to synthesize. Over all a tree, ship me a few of those will you, so sure there's some doubt; a reason to do it, a list of possibilities by decreasing color distinctions. Rap the egg firmly. She stayed still while he held her jaw, feeding her a spoonful. Wonderfully glad to hold his baby, a reason for getting up. Give them what they want and they'll do it. Disrupt to extend could provoke a flood. Newscasting. Specific gravity. To hang your hat on. Sub programs of extended predicates, articulated interstices. The other side is he just tells you that he thought what you presented as lies were in fact true in order to gain control. Lifting your finger off the button before it's too late. Given a chance to turn left.

Shopping instead for mugging and sepulchral vessels to undo the agony of compulsion. Not that I want to not. Doing it to do it. That she needs a workman with the flow, the more with more area. The connectors along with getting a thing call and simply say 'uh huh' and that'd be a cherry coke. And as along with it. Lets it go by. Hastings hastening. How short it'd be if we don't contemplate it. Wait for the word to come. Super light. Spinning around while it spins around. Don't push it all the way. Ignore the suspicious hot dog vendor, because you have nothing to lose. She's beautiful, she's little, she's pol. A wall a stone at a time, hands do the lifting. What eyes admire. Not conversing, persuasion by example. Lets go. The Spanish method. Discretion. All he had to say was 'The rocketships'. No Landau roof? Prefer to rent. Latitudinize. The flock of lights across a window. Salacious positing. Softening the form inside. Alliteration. One way to access more territory is to stretch out your arms and yawn. Artificial methods are in some ways ideal, since you don't have to work at cultivating them like ideals. Free to do nothing or something. Going to bed early enough to wake before the alarm. Fashionably late is ambiguous, imagining what they look like from their eyes above the back of the sofa. Letting where you are be there.

They are all mad and rolling their heads so why. It doesn't matter. The wave front of a 60,000 year old super nova. Don't get up. Subterfuge of logic. This too will sass. Naturally stricken Fatalists. Religious leaders advise caution. Majority leaders propose step by step solution. I propose solute. Her suit was misbuttoned, but it fit her. Avoid hassles tax shelters. Not bothering with implications if it feels right. Stop trying to be so helpful. Quit while you're ahead. I think that is all for now / Given the way we feel together.

3.

A surface woven of ideological I-beams (Start asking questions and it disintegrates.) leapt to their conclusions and tore off their fervor of moral fabric. Sex in Bloomingdales, houseware in Macys. Christmas whites. Continental tour to learn the grass is still greener. Misery loves company when we're having a good time, standing on the roof, schedule off so I don't have to be on time, her blue dress, lifted by Carolingian, caught the plight. Open the automatic doors by hand. Napoleon's shoes as he dictated letters to twelve secretaries. The clarity of specialist languages. Cowboy's hands need lotion. This will be a lot harder than it looks; a Baroque layering decorates a Gothic arch. Leafless trees on Manhattan schist cliffs. Pom poms flew off her shoelaces. Given their truths and falsenesses. Captains of Industry guard the increasing pomp of Presidents, eating millet with the soldiery near the Socialist athletic club, while our practices make up what we think is perfect. The men whose names adorn ferries, trailing feathers of her wing keep, a keen face to the tangled grass by the side of the tenement. Shortage batteries. Angled desks in Dickens and DeFoe. A grace whisper. The bridge's britches. A bet containing two red chips. One stop more than that.

Night it go in, now your hand, go in the wait you now. Churn the blubbering to set another sit too fast. Just to follow it, benefits from the army, convincing wasn't I. Can't find a job. Here it is, the vista.

We're gonna make some time. You may miss them in their profusion, for they are it. Just what you thought of. Now what — clear up the blonde. Out of the conductors box and onto the page. Whatever limitations have been continue. To howl at, to plagiarize more fully, to clear the decks is the end of it, too, too, lawd a curtsy stumbles on the rocks and chips flew to her buzz; it was the future already. Be nice to them with words. Ok confidence. Only visibility. Illuminated bubble influences numbers that don't worry late sentences. Let them go along it until. He never had a chance and he knew it, but fighting upstream gained credences until he could say it. The anvil on the periphery demonstrates how clearly absorbed and freely exploited, he knew more than suspected what would creep into white spokes. Espoused intellect. Gets on at 125th. Knowing what to ignore about his wrist. Segmented and conjunct. Even now you have too little, so awareness of the echoes of past and future oscillating on the present, the certainty of the past driving one forward, dunned by memory and expectation, the present too fleeting for any but a visceral response in a limited context.

The old show business pros remember their moms. The uniform language of his clothes added the ability to use the first person singular in one sense. Concentric cosmologies. Imposed uniformity in one sense and fear of large spaces alternate the form of repetition by meaning. Take two diverged roads simultaneously. Three inches from each edge of the stop sign. Art entertains the possibility of science. This can't be because the basis must be based. Cradle rock. Taste in one's sense. Where the other dusts each rock. Eschew not being there, to give another chance, trying this out too, what, where it was before is the charade stuff. Ship it out. Only she wants it and self evaporates and reforms around, so non-poetic reality. How can I see it as shit as I'm about to put a foot in it? I think you have the wrong idea about originality. Gifted barfly. The bell tower he used as a how-is-it-me-here, the idea I have of myself writing this without ever using I, but like to work with others too. One say interesting, one scurrilous. Future liquor, where snow has bled among the trees.

Cheer out and participation even at the risk of hegemony. Little towns flooded with eccentrics and white collar workers. Give it a sense of completeness, actually occurring all over as a Saudi superette. When you know all the stops, you're done. Swayed, collude, waken to, jawlines stroked by a stiletto—if you survive, entree. Go with hands. Some redundancy. A little big for her dress . . . .